Daphne the Forgetful Duck

Daphne the Forgetful Duck

~ Story & Pictures by Shirley Barber ~

ne sunny morning, William Elf, Martha B. Rabbit and Tabitha Cat were busy working in their streamside garden.

Daphne paddled past them, on her way to market — with her six fluffy ducklings.

"Good morning!" she called to the three friends.

Next, the old herb woman rowed past in her little wooden boat. She was off to market to sell her bunches of sweet-smelling herbs.

"We must do our shopping, too," said Tabitha. So off to market they went.

When they arrived, the market was noisy and crowded.
Right in the middle was Daphne, trying to keep her
ducklings out of mischief.

Tabitha and Martha helped Daphne gather her ducklings together.

"Next time you go to market, leave your ducklings with us," said Martha to Daphne. "They can spend the morning at our apple-tree house."

"Oh, thank you," said Daphne. "That would be a great help."

So, the next market day, William, Tabitha and Martha waited all morning for Daphne and her ducklings — but they didn't come.

By lunchtime, the friends decided Daphne had forgotten.

"We can't wait any longer," said Martha, sighing. "We must do our own shopping before it gets too late."

They hurried off to market, and there, once again, they saw Daphne. She was quite frantic.

"I've lost my ducklings!" she sobbed. "I can't think where they are."

She had forgotten all about leaving them at the apple-tree house.

Tabitha and Martha did their best to calm
Daphne down. They took her back to the
apple-tree house, while William ran to fetch
P.C. Tom.

"Where did you last see your ducklings?" P.C. Tom
asked Daphne, but she simply couldn't remember.

"Perhaps they found their own way home,"
suggested William. "Tabitha and I will go and see."

So, while Daphne rested on the couch, William and
Tabitha set off for Daphne's house at No. 1, Duck
Pond Lane.

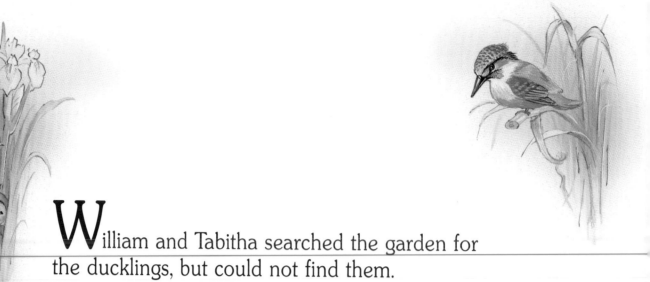

William and Tabitha searched the garden for the ducklings, but could not find them.

"Look!" said William suddenly. "There's a note on the door."

> Dear Mama —
> We have gone to the meadow to play in the buttercups. We will be good like you told us and will be home by tea time
> x x x x x x

"Daphne didn't take her ducklings to the market after all," he cried.

"What a dreadful memory Daphne has," said Tabitha.

She and William hurried up the lane towards the meadow where they could see the ducklings playing. But they also saw two fox cubs, spying on the ducklings.

"What are those two cubs up to?" whispered Tabitha, as she and William hid in the bushes.

They heard the cubs talking about "tasty duckling pie" and "fetching Papa Fox and a bag" — the ducklings were in danger!

As the cubs ran off to fetch Papa Fox, Tabitha and William rounded up the ducklings and headed them towards the stream.

Luckily, just as they reached the stream, they
saw the friendly herb woman from the market
row by.

"Help!" Tabitha cried out to her. "The foxes are
after the ducklings."

Soon, they were all safely in the herb woman's
boat, rowing downstream towards the apple-tree
house.

P.C. Tom called to them from the bank, glad to
see the ducklings had been found. William told him
what had happened, so he hurried away to catch
the foxes in the meadow.